Anne Rooney does not eat meat, in case the taste of blood becomes too appealing.

When not writing books she haunts the cemeteries and catacombs of Paris and Venice and raises non-vampiric daughters and chickens in Cambridge. She studied at a haunted college and her first car was a haunted van; the undead hold no fears for her.

With thanks to Kate and Hannah Frew,
Mary Hoffman, Shahrukh Husain and Juliet Wesley.

Drop Dead, Gorgeous

by Anne Rooney
www.annerooney.co.uk

Published by Ransom Publishing Ltd.
Unit 7, Brocklands Farm, West Meon, Hants. GU32 1JN, UK
www.ransom.co.uk

ISBN   978 184167 161 1

First published in 2012
Reprinted 2013, 2021

Vampire
Dawn

Drop Dead,
Gorgeous

ANNE ROONEY

Ransom

The Story So Far

Hungary, August ...

Juliette, Omar, Finn, Ruby and Alistair find a dead body in the forest ...

... Twenty-four hours later, they tie the murderer, Ava, to a tree, as one by one they fall sick ...

... When they wake, they are vampires, and that murderer looks rather appealing ...

... Mysterious nobleman Ignace, 400 years old and more sophisticated than is good for him, prevents them snacking on her ...

... But that dead body isn't as dead as it looked ...

... They go to Ignace's castle for a crash-course in being a modern vampire.

And so their adventures begin.

This is Juliette's story ...

One

Becca's knife clattered onto the table and a bead of blood glinted on her finger. Juliette froze. It was the first time she'd seen blood since becoming a vampire. She clutched the edge of the table so hard that her knuckles turned white.

'Ouch!' Becca raised her cut finger to her mouth. Juliette found herself leaning across the table towards her, longing for the blood.

'Didn't your mum ever tell you not to play with knives?' Charlie asked, as she handed Becca a tissue.

'It's OK, it's nothing,' Becca said. The blood was gone, but Juliette still felt faint with need.

'Are you all right?' Becca asked her, putting a hand over Juliette's white knuckles.

'I – I don't like the sight of blood,' Juliette whispered. 'It makes me feel ... faint.'

'Since when?' Charlie asked. 'It never used to bother you.'

'Since Hungary,' Juliette said quietly. She relaxed her grip on the table as the desperate urge to snatch at Becca's hand and drain it of blood started to fade.

'What happened to you in Hungary?' Charlie

asked, but Juliette just looked at the menu.

'Well?' Charlie persisted. 'You've been – well, strange. Ever since you got back.'

'Was it that boy – Omar? Is that his name? The cute one?' Becca tried.

'Are we going to eat?' Juliette said, ignoring their questions. In the time they had spent in his castle after the incident, Ignace had banned them all from discussing what had happened.

A woman at a table by the window watched them. Juliette stared her down, but there was something about her that didn't feel quite right. She sat with a much younger, very beautiful man. Juliette tried to hear what they were saying, but it was in a foreign language.

Becca and Charlie ordered pizza, but Juliette asked for just a glass of water and a diet cola.

'What's wrong with you?' Becca asked. 'You used to love pizza! We came here as your treat – you can't just have water!'

'But I'm going to Paris tomorrow,' Juliette said. 'I can't eat pizza the day before a photo shoot – I'll look bloated.'

Since Juliette's modelling had really taken off, Becca and Charlie were the only friends who still treated her in the same way – still going out, up for a laugh, neither envious nor slimy. She loved them more than ever, but now she couldn't share her greatest secret with them.

Becca watched as Juliette poured powder from a sachet into her glass of water and stirred it. The mix turned to a deep red goo.

'That stuff looks foul,' Becca said. 'It's like chewy blood – how can you eat it?'

'Meal replacement stuff,' Juliette said. 'It's not bad.'

Ignace, her vampire mentor, sent her supplies of ProVamp as powder. It had all the components of human blood that she needed. ProVamp was the only way to control her urge to bite. Most vampires used it in capsule form, but for Juliette the powder was easier – so many models took meal-replacement powders that it went unnoticed.

As she sipped the thick liquid, the tension from wanting Becca's blood slipped away.

'So – blood goop and diet cola?' Becca smiled,

finishing her pizza. 'And you say models are normal? Durrr.'

But Juliette wasn't listening. The woman at the corner table stared quite openly now, and didn't look away when Juliette glowered at her. Instead, she twisted her wedding ring on her finger, staring back. Was she married to this impossibly young, good-looking boy? Why should Juliette care about these two strangers? It made her uncomfortable, though. The woman seemed to ooze anger at her.

'Let's go,' Juliette said loudly.

The woman wrote in the mist on the window next to her with a finger.

'LEAVE MY HUSBAND ALONE.'

Juliette shrugged at her. She'd never seen the

woman before, or the young man.

Becca followed her gaze.

'You messing with that lady's husband?' she whispered, amused. 'If that's him, I can see why you would.'

'No!' said Juliette. And then louder, so the woman could hear, 'I have no idea who she is – or her husband. And I'm not messing with anyone. If only!'

The girls giggled.

The woman untied her silk scarf and flicked a look at Juliette – a *'Look at me'* look. Juliette looked away; the woman obviously thought she was someone else.

As the woman removed the scarf, the flash of its colour pulled Juliette's gaze back to her. She'd uncovered a tattoo on her neck: a red bow. Juliette's stomach lurched. She knew what that tattoo meant; Ignace had one. It was the mark of the guillotine, worn as a mark of respect for dead friends. In the French Revolution, thousands had been beheaded on the guillotine. Their relatives went to Victim Balls, wearing red ribbons like a line of blood around their necks. The tattoo was a permanent memorial.

Juliette couldn't look away from the woman now. It was two hundred years since the French Revolution. Only one type of person still alive could have been to a Victim Ball: a vampire.

Cold sweat prickled Juliette's back. She grabbed her coat and ran from the restaurant, Charlie and Becca hurrying to catch up with her.

Two

Juliette waited for Ignace to come online.

As her mentor, he helped her manage her need for blood, keep her vampirism hidden, and adjust to her new life. She had to tell him each day what she was doing, but it wasn't a chore. They shared a close bond, and she looked forward to checking in with him on iVamp.

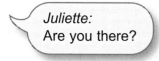

Juliette:
Are you there?

Ignace:
Yes. What are you doing?

Juliette:
I'm off to Paris tomorrow for a photo shoot
– as long as Mum will let me go.

Ignace:
Why wouldn't she?

Juliette:
Because she thinks I've got an eating disorder.
It's a problem. If the crew think I have, they
won't use me and my agent will send me to
rehab.

Ignace:
But you're beautiful. What alerted her?

Juliette:
Thank you ☺ She sees I don't eat. BTW I
saw a vampire woman. In Pizza Express.

Ignace:
They get everywhere. You've learned to
spot them? Good! Can I see you before
you go to Paris? Or in Paris?

> *Juliette:*
> I'd like that. But I thought you were in Hungary? I'm getting the Eurostar at 6. Can we meet in Paris?

> *Ignace:*
> Of course. I can get to Paris. BTW how did you recognise the vampire?

'Juliette!' her mother called up the stairs.

> *Juliette:*
> I have to go – I'll message you later xx

She snapped her laptop shut and moved to the door. Far away, in his warm library, Ignace looked at those two 'x's and his heart sang.

* * * * *

St Pancras was crowded, bustling with people wet from the rain outside. Mrs Grigson pursed her lips, trying to press the pastries she'd bought into her daughter's hands.

'I really don't want them,' Juliette said.

'You never eat anything. Please, just have a couple to eat on the train. For me?'

'No – I'll be sick.'

'That's exactly what I'm worried about!' Mrs Grigson said.

Even looking at the package made Juliette's stomach turn.

'It's not true what they say – that you can't be too rich or too thin,' her mother said. 'Your father's too rich and you're too thin. I, sadly, am neither.'

'I'm not too thin,' Juliette responded. She refused to rise to her mother's challenge to discuss her father. 'I'm just right. That's why they want me in Paris.'

'You're turning into one of those size-zero models, all skin and bones and sicking up your guts every day,' her mother hissed.

'I don't have bulimia, Mum; I just don't want any pastries.'

'I've heard you being sick,' her mother whispered.

'Look, I have to go,' Juliette said, taking the pastries. 'I'll miss the train.'

She kissed her mother goodbye, stuffed her ticket into the machine and hurried through the barrier.

Juliette scanned the security queue for people she recognised. She knew most of the photographers now, and many of the models – though some of the girls were difficult, envious of her success. She just closed her brittleness around her like a metal cloak and let their hostility bounce off.

This time, she couldn't see anyone she knew. She smiled to herself and relaxed.

She settled into her seat in first class and sent a text to Ignace: *'See you at Gare du Nord, 7:30 x'*.

When the waitress came, Juliette ordered a glass of champagne and sat flicking through *Vogue*.

It was a pose; she was playing at being the glamorous model. More often she played Angry Birds on her phone and sat eating Monster Munch with her legs curled up underneath her.

But there wouldn't be Monster Munch any more – or marshmallows or fizzy pineapple cubes. No more normal food.

Today she wanted to feel grown up, wanted to look as if she was in control, even though she didn't feel it. She'd felt out of control since coming back from Hungary, and she hated it.

Three

Two hours later, the train slid into the Gare du Nord and Juliette scanned the faces on the platform for Ignace. He wasn't there. Her heart turned to lead in her chest.

And suddenly there he was, coming up the escalator from the Métro, dressed in a long, black, tailored coat and charcoal-grey trousers. She watched him for a couple of minutes. He was beautiful. He moved with such poise. And he was searching the crowds, clearly eager to see her. The heavy feeling in her chest dissolved.

Juliette smiled, raised a hand, then decided instead to watch him find her. His brow furrowed – he couldn't see her. And then he grinned and hurried towards her.

She wanted to run, to leap into his arms, but she just quickened her pace until at last he drew her towards him. She leaned forwards, about to offer her cheek, but he kissed her full on the lips. It took her breath away.

'Juliette.'

It wasn't what she'd expected, but she thrilled at his touch. They stood there, hands on each other's arms, for a long time, just looking.

She hadn't seen him since she'd left Budapest at the end of August, but she'd spoken to him online every day. They'd come to know each other so well. She felt so drawn to him, so safe.

At last, they linked arms and walked out into the cold dark of Paris in November. A light rain fell. He hurried her into a taxi and gave the name of a bar near her hotel.

Inside, a mournful saxophone played while they drank black coffee and looked at each other. It was less than twenty-four hours since she'd been messing about with Becca and Charlie in Pizza Express, and here she was in a different world.

'It's so good to see you,' he said at last. 'I hadn't realised – how good it would be.'

He reached across the table and touched her hand. Juliette didn't trust herself to speak. She hadn't allowed herself to think of this possibility, but she had wanted it. In her dreams, sleeping and waking, he was always there, looking after her. And more.

She took his hand, and he leaned over and kissed her again, a long, lingering kiss that made her skin prickle.

'So tell me,' he said, 'about the photo shoot. About what you will be doing.' And the moment was over and she told him the plan.

'But this will sell clothes? Pictures of a woman spattered with mud – albeit a beautiful woman?'

He smiled, and she did, too. Not only was modern fashion an alien world because he was a

man, it was an alien world because he was four
hundred years old.

When she had to go, he held her hand again
and looked deep into her eyes.

'I'm glad I came. Even for just this hour. I
needed to see you again, to know you're safe. To
hold you. And to kiss you.'

He kissed her again, and her head swam away,
as it had done when she'd seen Becca's blood, but
this time there was no ProVamp to steady her.

'Are you going home to Hungary now?' she
asked.

'Yes. Then to Russia. But perhaps I'll stay a day
or two, just to be near you.'

'Where will you stay?'

'There are places, people to stay with.'

'How will I find you?'

'Will you need to?' He smiled.

She didn't answer, not wanting to give away how much she might need to. Instead, she leaned across the table and gave him a short, chaste kiss on the lips and then pushed back her chair and left the bar without looking back.

Outside, the cold air stung her face and made her eyes water.

four

All the crew were in the same hotel. It was good enough – shabby around the edges, but comfortable.

Juliette's room had a shuttered window that opened onto a tiny courtyard filled with stone pots that spilled ivy over old, cracked tiles. When she woke, the edges of the ivy leaves were traced with frost – a cold day for modelling flimsy wisps of summer dresses.

By seven o'clock everyone was in the breakfast room. Juliette had black coffee and a sachet of ProVamp with hot water. Lots of the models had meal-replacement powders – though for most it was for weight control, not an alternative to human blood. She ate it with a spoon, holding the mug close to her mouth to hide the blood-red colour.

Juliette sent a text to Becca, folding herself over her phone so the others wouldn't notice she had no one to talk to.

'Know what I said about not messing with anyone? Looks like that's changing! Can't wait to tell you. Call tonight? xx'

Soon, they were all on the banks of the River Seine, the wind whipping chiffon against goose-bumped arms. Between shots, the models huddled in jumpers, coats and blankets. Two others chain-smoked and gossiped in French, too quickly for Juliette to keep up.

Juliette sipped black coffee from a flask, legs dangling over the edge of the quay above the slimy mud. A small tangle of passers-by stopped on a bridge to watch the shoot – their glimpse of what they thought was a glamorous life.

'They don't have a clue, do they?' she said to the other two models. 'About our life. I mean, it's all mud and half-cold coffee and being freezing cold.' She laughed, inviting them to agree with her.

One of the girls shrugged. She didn't speak English. The other laughed briefly then turned away. Juliette played with her phone again, pretending to be busy, pretending not to know or care that they didn't want her there. There was no reply from Becca yet.

A couple stayed on the bridge, watching longer than the rest. The woman was elegant with dark hair cropped short like Carey Mulligan, wearing sunglasses even in the pale, winter sun. A younger man hung on her arm like a Christmas bauble. He was fit, though – Juliette could tell that even at a distance. She felt the memory of Ignace's kiss on her lips and smiled.

Juliette tried again with the other models.

'Who are those two?'

One shrugged again. Juliette asked again, in French.

'Never seen them before,' one girl said. 'You're very young. You'll soon learn – all kinds of weirdos follow us around.'

'I've been doing this for two years,' Juliette said. 'I know about weirdos. But they've been watching for ages.'

The girl didn't reply.

In the afternoon they took one of the glass-roofed boats that carry tourists up and down the river. Shooting inside was much warmer. But then the art director wanted some shots with Juliette at the front of the boat, standing like a figurehead against the setting sun. Cold again.

'Only a few shots, darling,' the photographer pleaded. 'Fifteen minutes tops and you'll be back in the warm.'

It felt dangerous, but there was a flagpole to hold onto and the boat moved smoothly enough. A pretty young man helped the photographer carry his kit.

For the first shots, Juliette leaned back against the boat. Then the photographer told her to grip the pole and lean out. The young man wiped the flagpole with a rag.

'Eez all clean for mademoiselle,' he said, smirking. It irritated Juliette. She wasn't that prissy. Did even he have to mock her?

She stepped cautiously in her high heels, then grabbed the flagpole and swung herself round, leaning far over the dark water. The photographer snapped away, shouting encouragement. The wind stung her face, and the water rushed by below.

But suddenly her hands were burning. The young man smiled nastily as agony registered on her face.

She just had time to realise that he must have put something on the pole on purpose. The pain shot through her palms and fingers, blazed across her mind, and loosened her grip.

She let go.

In a moment, the icy water snatched her from the air and pulled her under the moving boat.

five

The cold was so intense she couldn't think. Her mind emptied, and she was aware only of cold and calmness.

Is this how you drown? she thought at last.

The water pulled her, first down, then along. She let it carry her without a struggle. She didn't feel her lungs were bursting – she didn't even feel she needed to breathe. But as a vampire she barely breathed at all. She wondered how long she could stay under the water.

It seemed hours before she finally drifted to the surface. The lights of Paris glittered on the water and people on the boat waved their arms and screamed – they were panicking for her.

Someone threw a white and red ring, but she saw it all as though it were happening to someone else. It didn't occur to her to try to save herself, to help in her own rescue.

Juliette breathed in the freezing air, and then the water tugged her under again. Her water-logged cardigan pulled her down, so she shrugged it off. It sank, and the water released her to the surface again.

Suddenly there was a face in front of hers, a face fringed by long, wet, red hair and filled by wide, frightened eyes and an open mouth. Hair fanned out around the girl's shoulders and Juliette thought briefly of mermaids.

The girl was shouting something at her, but it was in French and she was too confused to understand.

And then small hands were on her – the girl took Juliette's arm, then her shoulders, cupped a hand under her chin, and dragged her through the water. *It was like being a boat*, she thought dreamily. Not *on* a boat, but *being* a boat – just passing through the water without effort.

Soon she was hauled out, strong hands from the boat lifting and pulling her, and then she realised she was in trouble. She had to move. She had to make them know she was alive.

If they thought she was dead, they'd pummel her chest and try to force air into her lungs. They'd push a mouth against hers and blow into her, just as Omar had done when he thought Finn was dead in Hungary, before they knew they were vampires. Before they knew they only breathed a fraction as much as they used to.

It was the blood that did it. The scent of it cut through the fug in Juliette's mind. She didn't have to try, now. Her eyes opened and she scanned the faces around her, looking for the one who was bleeding.

The girl who had saved her raised her hand to her head, and there was a tiny line of red on it.

The girl spoke in French ...

'Ah, mon Dieu. Elle vive! Elle vive!'

There was a rush of voices, someone covered Juliette with a blanket and other hands put something under her head.

But all she could see was that delicious line of red. Her mind was running riot. She saw herself sitting up, reaching out to the girl, pulling the hand to her mouth, licking along the line of blood. Then pressing her lips hard to the hand and sucking, sucking, drawing out the blood ...

But she was too weak. Her head raged, but her body barely moved.

At last she pushed herself up on one elbow, parted her lips and leaned towards the girl. She was one of the models. She wiped her wet hands on the ruined dress, and so the blood was gone, smeared into a tiny pink stain on the drenched silk.

Juliette let herself fall back as the moment passed. She was freezing, and pulled the blanket close around her shoulders as her agent's voice broke through the crowd, filled with panic and concern.

'Juliette! Oh my goodness, what happened? Are you all right? Someone, get more blankets – and for the girl who saved her. Call an ambulance!'

'I'm fine,' Juliette said. 'I don't need an ambulance. I'm just cold and wet.'

She would not, *could not*, go to hospital. Everything would unravel if she went to the emergency department of an ordinary hospital.

In minutes Juliette's accident faded from deadly threat to an incident to be dealt with. She took the brandy she was offered, and the coats and jerseys piled around her.

The girl who had saved her had been wrapped in blankets and hustled away. Juliette didn't have a chance to thank her.

Six

Back in the hotel, Juliette stood for a long, long time in the shower, the hot water soaking out the cold that seemed to go right down to her bones.

The smirking face of the young man floated in front of her eyes. Why had he tried to hurt her? She was unpopular on the shoot, but that was a dangerous prank.

Or was it something more?

Her phone beeped as she got out of the shower. She seized it, dripping water onto the carpet, desperate to talk to Ignace. But it wasn't him – it was a message from a number she didn't know:

'I saw you at the river this morning. You're just the girl I'm looking for. Would you audition for my project? The art director gave me your number – hope you don't mind. Call or text any time.'

The professional rush made up for the disappointment that it wasn't Ignace. A year ago, she wouldn't have set up a meeting with someone she didn't know, bypassing her agent. But as a vampire she felt invincible – even after her scare on the river. Perhaps especially after her scare.

She texted straight back: 'OK. *See you in the hotel bar at 9.'*

An hour. She took a ProVamp capsule – she didn't want any distractions during the meeting. She wore a blood-red body-con dress, low heels, a slash of eye-liner and no jewellery. Simple but stunning – just what she needed to pitch for work.

She checked iVamp but Ignace wasn't online, so she left a message:

'Had an accident on the river during the photo shoot. Very shaken, but OK. Off to a meeting – more work! Talk later? xx'

She sent a second message to Becca, too:

'Where are you, lovely? I have gossip and no one to share it with! Text me! Love you xx'

As soon as Juliette walked into the bar, an elegant woman strode over to greet her with kisses to both cheeks. The woman wore large, dark sunglasses and had short black hair. Her dress had a high collar with a narrow slit at the front that showed creamy pearls against olive skin.

Mediterranean, Juliette thought, wealthy and stylish, but somehow not quite right for the fashion world. And there was something vaguely familiar about the woman, but she couldn't place her. It was the woman from the bridge, she was sure, but there was something else ...

Still, Juliette saw so many people – designers, magazine people, agents, photographers. Their paths could have crossed anywhere.

The woman introduced herself as Titania.

'Have you ever considered acting?' she asked, and Juliette felt the familiar sharp pang of excitement.

'All models have considered acting,' she replied coolly, 'but few get to do it.'

'Well, perhaps you will. Can I get you a drink?'

'Mineral water, please.' She wanted cola, but it seemed childish.

'Ah, of course. You models – never eating or drinking anything.'

They shared an overpriced bottle of water as Titania told her about the project.

She was making a film, she said, set during the French Revolution. She needed to get the backing of a big studio and so needed some presentation material. Would Juliette screen test? she asked.

Of course she would! Juliette's thoughts raced along a well-trodden path to fame.

Juliette squeezed her hands together under the table, trying to hide her excitement. Titania smiled.

'You should be excited; it could be the start of something big – for both of us.'

Juliette wanted to ask *'why me?'* but knew it was a bad idea. Still, there was something about Titania that made her feel ... she wasn't sure: not *nervous*, but slightly uneasy. But Juliette couldn't afford to say 'no' to this.

They arranged to meet the next afternoon.

* * * * *

Back in her room, Juliette wondered why Titania hadn't approached her through her agent, Chris. She buzzed Chris on her mobile, but got no answer.

Seven

Juliette's hands were still sore the next morning. She thought again of the handsome young man who'd wiped the flagpole and sneered so nastily when she was hurt. There had been something slightly familiar about him – she'd seen him before, she was sure, but where?

But there was no time to think about it now; she'd tell Ignace later.

The second day's shoot was at least partly indoors, in and around the cathedral of Notre Dame. Some of the other models whispered together and pointed at her, no doubt talking about her ordeal. A girl with a torrent of flame-coloured hair offered Juliette a cigarette, which she refused.

'Eez cool, no? The ball gowns, the stone monsters?' the girl said. 'I am Agnès. You?'

'Juliette.' She smiled, thankful for the girl's kindness. And then she realised.

'It was you, wasn't it? Who saved me from the river. Thank you so much. I didn't have a chance at the time ... '

'No worry,' Agnès said. Then a photographer called her away. She shrugged and went with him.

They all wore artfully ripped silk and lace dresses and draped themselves over the ancient stones of the cathedral of Notre Dame. It thrilled Juliette, and she was bursting to tell someone, but she couldn't tell Becca.

She sent a message to Omar – *'I'm a vampire in a ball gown in an old church in Paris: you couldn't make it up! xx'*

He replied straight away: *'Cool – wish I was there to see. Tell me about it some time? xxx'*

Immediately, she felt bad. Omar liked her – he had done in Hungary. That message had looked like encouragement, but now she could only think of Ignace.

After the photo shoot, Juliette returned to the hotel for a shower before the screen test. She decided not to tell Chris about it. He'd want lots of paperwork, and it just wasn't worth the hassle. And he didn't want her to do film – he wanted her to stay in modelling, earning good money for his agency.

* * * * *

Juliette couldn't get hold of Ignace, so she sent him a text with the address Titania had given her, just to be safe, and got into a taxi.

The taxi pulled up outside a large, old house in a smart area. It had once been grand, but the stone was crumbling, and the plants that clung to the walls seemed to be pulling it apart. The huge iron door knocker was shaped like a gloved fist ready to thump the wood. Titania opened the door almost as soon as Juliette dropped the knocker.

'Juliette, how good to see you!'

She introduced the rest of the crew, and Juliette recognised some of them. A crowd of models, male and female, chatted and joked in period costume. She was pleased to see Agnès, who waved a white-gloved hand as Juliette came in. She need not have worried; it looked like a properly run project.

A stylist arrived carrying a bundle of huge dresses, stiff with starch, petticoats and hoops, and frothy with lace. She helped Juliette into a powder-blue silk gown dripping with cream lace and so wide that she would have to turn sideways to walk through a door. Make-up took half an hour. Her reflection showed a ghostly pale face with a couple of velvet beauty spots and an ornate white wig. Juliette wondered what Ignace would make of her in these clothes from the time of his youth. Thinking of him, she checked her phone for messages:

'DON'T GO. *You're not totally invincible, but you are totally precious. xx*'

Two kisses. She remembered his lips, her mind drifting while the stylist pinned and sprayed the wig.

Why not go? It was obviously OK here. He was being over-protective, and it made her smile.

The first task was easy. They danced, drank wine, flirted and talked and leaned against the striped silk walls while the photographers and cameraman circled, snapping and filming. Everything was perfectly beautiful – if it weren't for the lights and the cables trailing across the floor, she could have believed she really was in the eighteenth century, dancing the night away with Ignace – maybe even at a real Victim Ball.

He'd been there, had lived in Paris from 1784 and had witnessed the Revolution and the Terror. He'd told her how he'd seen cartload after cartload of his aristocratic friends dragged to the guillotine and beheaded. And he'd shown her the red bow tattooed on the side of his neck.

She felt suddenly guilty at playing at being one of those victims. Agnès glided past, squeezing Juliette's arm on the way, and Juliette felt calmer.

After an hour, Titania called a halt and told most of the models and crew they could leave or relax. Juliette hurried over to talk to Agnès, but Titania caught her arm and drew her aside.

'We're going to do a little scene outside. Will you help, Juliette? I'd love it if you would. You'll need to change out of the ball gown, I'm afraid.'

Titania was also in costume, a deep crimson gown decorated with gold. Juliette examined her elegant Mediterranean face, the clear skin of her throat – and the tattoo of a tiny red bow. She felt suddenly hollow and light-headed.

That's why Titania looked familiar – she was the woman from Pizza Express, the one who'd told her to stay away from her husband. Her grip on Juliette's arm was firm. Too firm.

Already Titania had led her through tall glass doors into a courtyard and Juliette gasped at what she saw in front of her.

Eight

A tall wooden frame with, at the top, a wedge of blade hanging from a rope – a guillotine. At the bottom, there was a wooden neck brace and a long board tilted upwards. And beyond the board, a basket to catch the head, and a box to hold the discarded body. Juliette took it all in.

'Is it real?' she whispered.

Titania shrugged.

'I have no idea – I just ordered it and it came. But don't worry – we aren't going to cut anyone's head off!' She laughed, a sudden, brittle sound that reminded Juliette of breaking glass.

Titania turned to the beautiful young man who hadn't left her side all afternoon. Now they were in the light, Juliette recognized him, too. He was the man who'd wiped the flagpole. But he was also the man from Pizza Express, and from the bridge. Titania's husband?

Juliette's mouth dried up and she felt cold sweat on her back. She remembered the warning: *'Keep away from my husband'*. Why? What did he have against her?

Juliette didn't want to be there any more. Titania had stalked her. Why else had she been in

London, and then Paris? Why not just go to Juliette's agent, or look at her portfolio online?

'Darling, please show everyone how it works.'

Titania patted the young man's arm. He stepped up to the guillotine and used a lever to release the rope. Juliette jumped as the blade plunged at lightning speed. But it shuddered to a halt just above the neck brace, stopped by two large metal spikes driven into the frame.

'See?' said Titania. 'It's not a real blade, and anyway there are stops to prevent it falling far enough even to bruise. It's so safe I would use my own child for this shot.'

Juliette flinched. How could anyone say such a thing? Titania saw her expression change. She raised an eyebrow, and something glinted in her eyes. Juliette looked away quickly. She felt sick and wanted to leave.

But the door to the ballroom was blocked by camera equipment and Titania still held her arm. No way out.

'Alain, my darling – would you mind showing our new friend just how safe it is? Alain is very dear to me. I wouldn't do this if it weren't *totally* safe.'

Alain pulled on the rope to haul the blade back up and secured it. One of the actors strapped him face down on the tilting board, lowered it so that his head was in place, and fitted the neck brace.

Juliette held her breath as Titania herself released the lever. The blade juddered onto the stops again. Alain, unhurt, laughed as the actor helped him from the board. Juliette looked again at the blocked doorway.

'Now,' said Titania, 'aristocrats weren't executed

in their ball gowns, so let's go back to wardrobe. After we've done these last shots, we'll all share a glass of champagne and toast our little venture.'

Titania led her by the arm back inside and watched while the make-up artist transformed Juliette into a bedraggled and filthy prisoner.

'If you were really going to the guillotine, they'd slice your beautiful hair off,' Titania said. 'For the film, you'll have a short wig, but for now we'll just tie it.'

Juliette stared in the mirror at her face – frightened, dirty, and unfamiliar. Her shift was grey and itchy.

'Lovely, darling!' Titania said. 'You'll be finished in moments. Come.'

Juliette glanced around the crowded room. She

was being silly. It couldn't be dangerous with all these people here. She sent a quick text to Ignace, asking him to meet her later: *'Just doing a shoot with a guillotine! Can you meet me at 8? I'm leaving Paris tomorrow ☹ xx'.*

He replied immediately with a simple question *'Where are you?'* She'd already given him the address, so she just called up the earlier message. Titania was looking impatient. *'Must go – Titania waiting,'* she added, before pressing *Send*.

'Leave that here,' Titania said, snatching the phone from her. 'There were no phones in 1793!'

As Juliette walked away, her phone started to ring. Titania dropped it onto the make-up table and followed Juliette outside. The phone rang and rang, but Juliette had gone.

Nine

The courtyard was eerily empty, with only one photographer and the executioner, who had his back to her. The spotlights glinted off the guillotine blade.

'We needed space to get the lights and cameras in the right place for these shots,' Titania explained. 'We can rejoin everyone else in five minutes when we're done.' Strains of eighteenth-century music filtered through the doors from the chateau. Inside, she saw Agnès the other side of the room, drinking champagne and laughing.

'Just a couple of shots,' Titania said breezily.

Juliette, bare-foot and shivering in the freezing November air, stepped up to the bench. Someone – it must have been the executioner – snatched her hands and pulled them behind her back, then tied them with a harsh rope. Juliette cried out in surprise and alarm. She panicked, wriggling her arms uselessly.

'Stop!' she shouted. 'I'm not ready! I don't want to!'

The executioner pushed her against the tilting board and brought up his knee to keep her there, as he wrapped the leather straps around her body.

She tried to struggle, but it was useless. She was soon securely strapped.

'No!' she shouted. 'Let me go!'

She looked up as the board tilted forwards. The blade looked different, heavier. Perhaps it was the light. She glanced at the frame, to see the reassuring metal pins.

They were gone.

Panic erupted from her.

'No!' she screamed. 'Don't do it! I don't want to! Let me go!'

She struggled vigorously but the straps held her close to the board.

Titania smiled.

'Excellent, yes! Keep struggling. That's very convincing,' she said. Juliette twisted and thrashed, but she was held firmly. The neck brace came down. She looked down into the basket.

'Wait!' she cried. 'Stop filming! I don't want to do it!'

'Come on,' said Titania, 'let's do it quickly and we can go in the warm.' She sounded irritated.

'I don't want to!' Juliette shouted. 'It looks different. Please. Wait a moment.'

'Don't be childish!' snapped Titania. 'I thought you were grown-up enough for this job.'

Juliette heard the door to the courtyard click closed and looked across, but could see only a dark shape in the shadows. Someone had got in – why couldn't she have got out when there was still time?

'Please – could you show me again that it's safe? Just the once?' It had been half an hour at least – plenty of time for someone to fiddle with it. Buy why would they? It was ridiculous, she knew. She twisted her head, trying to see the man holding the rope.

She finally saw the executioner's face. It was Alain. Juliette couldn't have been more horrified. Panic rose in her throat and she was sure she would be sick.

'Please – s'il vous plait,' she tried, 'show me again with someone else.'

'Is that really necessary?' asked Titania with a sigh that sounded as much bored as impatient.

'I think it's an excellent idea.'

Ignace! He stepped from the shadows by the door and Juliette's heart leapt. Titania blanched, her lips shrank to a thin, straight line, and her eyes hardened. They were the colour of the guillotine blade, Juliette noticed. Not beautiful – cold, hard. Evil. Twisting her head to watch Ignace and Titania hurt her neck.

'Perhaps, Alain – is it? – would do the honours, and you can drop the blade, Titania.' Ignace spat the name. Juliette had never heard him angry, and this was pure venom. Titania stared at him with hatred.

'That is not necessary,' she said.

'Oh, I think it is. Very necessary,' said Ignace. 'The girl deserves to be reassured, don't you think? Alain, please.'

Titania moved to stop him, but Alain was already helping Juliette out of the way. He set the board flat and lay down on it. He didn't need to be strapped – he trusted Titania. Juliette felt foolish.

'You don't need to! This man has no power here!' Titania shouted at Alain. Juliette looked from Ignace to Titania, confused and afraid. She backed away from the guillotine towards Ignace's outstretched arm, which he immediately wrapped around her protectively. Titania and Ignace stared at each other across the guillotine. The cameraman helped Alain with the neck brace.

'So, if it's perfectly safe, let your toy-boy try it again,' Ignace said. 'That's all right, isn't it – Titania?'

She glowered at him.

'Lovers' tiff,' muttered the cameraman, shrugging. 'Call me when they're ready.'

He went back into the chateau and Ignace closed the door behind him, taking the key from the inside and locking it.

Juliette suddenly felt freezing cold. Lovers' tiff? Ignace and Titania? How could that be?

'Don't do it!' Titania suddenly screamed.

'Problem, Titania?' Ignace was cool, calm. Incredibly sexy, Juliette thought. 'He wouldn't have lasted long anyway – sixty years at most, but not to your taste after another ten. Unless ... You didn't bite him, did you? There's only one way to be sure, isn't there? Will he bleed? Let the blade fall, Titania.'

Titania put her hand on the release lever. 'This is a stage guillotine. I would bet my life on it. This is unnecessary.'

'Will you bet *his* life on it?'

Ignace suddenly reached into his pocket, pulled out two ProVamp capsules and stuffed one into Juliette's mouth and the other into his own.

'Swallow!' he said. She did so, choking as it caught in her throat.

Titania looked directly into Ignace's eyes, a look of pure defiance. Or hatred. Her hand was still on the release handle.

'I trust you,' Alain said. He reached up to put his hand on her arm – and the blade fell. All the way down.

Ten

The thud of Alain's head landing in the basket would echo in Juliette's memory for five hundred years. His body sprawled on the board. Blood pooled on the cracked stone paving, but the horror barely touched her. Instead, she felt desire welling up inside her.

'Hold on,' said Ignace through gritted teeth. 'Hold on.'

Juliette was almost faint with her need for the blood. She struggled against Ignace's firm grip. In an instant, the urge became controllable as the capsule took effect. But Titania was unprepared for the torrent of blood. The look of anguish that transformed her face the moment the head fell into the basket was gone in seconds. Now, her hunger for Alain's blood was uncontrollable.

Juliette buried her face in Ignace's chest and let the vampire in her be quelled by the drugs. Soon, her human emotions resurfaced and she wept with horror at what had happened to Alain – and had so nearly happened to her. Ignace held her firmly.

When Titania raised her face, it was smeared with blood; Juliette felt sick to her stomach.

'So, my dear,' said Ignace. 'You hadn't bitten

him. It's good to see you have some restraint still – though for him the outcome was unfortunate. Your jealousy knows no bounds, does it? You'd have killed Juliette just to harm me. Yet she's done nothing to you.'

'Nothing! You're obsessed with her!' Titania screamed at him. 'You know the deal – only humans. No vampires. How dare you betray me with this little tart? And I warned her. She could have saved herself.'

Juliette pulled away from Ignace in horror, but he held her shoulders.

'You?' she gasped. 'You and her?'

'Didn't he tell you, pretty?' Titania sneered, her blood-smeared mouth turning up at the corners. 'I'm his wife, little Juliette. I tracked you down

from his iVamp logs, and you were too beautiful –
so I knew. He's a sucker for beautiful girls. I told
you, showed you my wedding ring, my tattoo –
but you didn't care. You should have cared.'

'I didn't know!' cried Juliette. 'He didn't tell me!'

'Surely you didn't think someone as great and
powerful as Ignace would really be in love with
you? We've been married for over 220 years. We
met during the French Revolution.' She indicated
the guillotine, the chateau. 'This was our home.'

'She will no doubt take great pleasure in telling
you,' added Ignace, 'that I was then Joseph-Ignace
Guillotin. I invented this device.'

'You what?' Juliette shook her shoulders free of
his hands.

'I invented the guillotine. They were beheading people in a horribly cruel way. The guillotine is quick, painless – an act of mercy. The French Revolution became a terrible purge of vampires – though you won't find that in the history books. I couldn't save them, but I made the end easier for them.'

'There's a certain justice to it, don't you think?' Titania grinned, a hideous, clown-like face of white skin with a huge, blood-stained mouth. Juliette couldn't have imagined anything more horrific.

'You see, Juliette, being married to the same person for all of eternity can be rather a struggle. Particularly if that person is Ignace. Can you imagine spending centuries with the same man? So marriage amongst vampires is more – shall we say – open.

But we agreed that we may each only take humans as lovers. Why? Because they'll be dead in a few decades, they're no long-term threat. But not you.' She spat the accusation with such venom that Juliette flinched. She was horribly out of her depth – why had she never asked Ignace about the last two centuries?

'I didn't know,' she said. 'I didn't know he was married – to you or anyone.' She looked at Ignace, torn, hurt, her eyes pleading for an explanation.

'It's a sham,' he said. 'No relationship can last centuries. Everything runs its natural course, whether it's in ten, twenty or two hundred years. It's time to move on, Titania.'

'You killed my boy,' Titania said.

'No, Titania. *You* killed your boy. And you would have killed her.' He laid a gentle hand on

Juliette's shoulder and Juliette did not shake it off. 'You know a vampire must not kill another vampire.'

'But it would have been such justice!' Titania said triumphantly. 'Your floozy killed with your own guillotine! And Alain would have done it, not me.'

Juliette shivered.

'A technicality,' Ignace said. 'He was just your tool.'

'Why did you let Alain die?' Juliette asked.

'I can get another. And I wouldn't let *him*' – Titania pointed at Ignace – 'make me look a coward. And so that you would both see what I would have done to you.'

'You can never back down, can you?' Ignace said bitterly.

The three of them looked at each other, and the headless body of Alain lay between them. *So this is how it's going to be*, Juliette thought.

'We need to get out of here,' Ignace said. 'This is a hell of a mess.'

'What about Alain?' Juliette asked. 'He did nothing. And he's dead.'

'He would have been dead in fifty years anyway,' Titania said. Juliette was ready to cry out at the inhumanity of it, but Ignace silenced her.

'Clean yourself up,' he ordered his wife. 'The police will come, you know that. It was a terrible accident. It has to be. We can't afford the publicity, people tracking us down, discovering our very long history. The stop fell out, and you dropped the lever by accident. You are distraught at the death of your lover. You always were a good actress. Act your way out of this.'

He took Juliette's hand. 'Get changed. We're leaving. I want you out of Paris. Tonight.'

'What will happen?' Juliette asked. 'What about the police?'

'They won't know you were here. This will be managed – it always is, it always will be. Things go wrong, and we fix them. We have friends in high places.'

Juliette let him take her hand and lead her back through the chateau. She kept her head bowed and didn't look even at Agnès. Back in the wardrobe section, she changed into her own clothes. Ignace ran a finger around her neck.

'Your neck is so lovely, and so precious,' he said. 'Let's keep it safe from now on.'

They went out into the street, where freezing rain was starting to fall, and Ignace somehow called a taxi from nowhere. He settled her into the back seat, and kissed her once.

'It always works out. You'll learn, in time. And you have a lot of time — we all do.'

The rain glittered on the window and Juliette hugged her knees to her chest and cried as the taxi pulled away. The blue wink of a police car rounded the corner and she saw Ignace raise his hand, waving to her, or the police car, or both.

She was out of sight before the police car reached the chateau.

Vampire Dawn

*The story starts with **Die Now or Live Forever**. Read it first.*

Then follow each individual's story. You can read these in any order:

Juliette's story

Finn's story

Omar's story

Alistair and Ruby's story

Ava's story

Plus an essential guide for new vampires.

Find out more at www.vampiredawn.co.uk. Follow the vampires on Facebook: www.facebook.com/VampireDawnBooks

twitter: @vampiredawn